TEMPORAL MALADIES AND REMEDIES

BY
DR. FELICITY
COSGROVE

Copyright © 2021 by Lauren Lyn
Cidell

ISBN: 978-0-9997515-0-3

Purple Haze, an imprint of Purple
Turkey Press
www.purpleturkeypress.com

First edition: September 2021

Cover design by Lauren Lyn Cidell

*Dedicated
to
Felix John Cosgrove,
My twin brother and
braver half*

Acknowledgements

This book would not have happened without the help and support of so many:

My Mentors
Nursing Sister Claire Gordon,
Dr. Diana Fielding, and
Professor Ezekiel Wood

My Colleagues:
Dr. Annie Talmadge, Dr. Sven Suddigrumpa, and Herbalist Svana Eirvinur

Thanks are also due to my editor Lauren Lyn Cidell and her fellow *Inklings*: Don Hunt, Wren Roberts, Chris Gerrib, Jason Evans, and Dex Greenbright

Editor's Note

The contents of this book are fictitious in nature, and solely intended for entertainment purposes.

Contents

Dr. Felicity Cosgrove

Preface

This book was written for the purpose of educating the general public. It is most certainly NOT a manual for self-diagnosis or self-medication. Nor is it an invitation to replicate any of the medicines which are herein described.°

In order to promote the better understanding of the

° Both the author and publisher hereby waive any liability for the irresponsible actions of others.

13

reader, it is necessary to provide some information as to the different methods of temporal voyaging. However, this does not include Temporamancy. That branch of wizardry is beyond the author's ken, as it is indeed beyond the ken of all except its own practitioners. Therefore, let us consider the most common methods: the vehicular, the vorticular, and the ventricular.

Temporal vehicles are twofold in nature: those that are self-propelled and those that are not. In the case of the former it is possible to voyage through space as well as time. As for the latter, such vehicles must either be transported to the physical site of the temporal destination, or its operator must venture there by some other means.

Vorticular voyaging requires the generation of a tachyon vortex through the aether. As entire monographs have been devoted to this subject as well as diverse papers, no more need be said here except to clarify that a tachyon vortex and a wyrmhole are not the same phenomenon.

Wyrms, those fabulous creatures known as dragons in the Far East, move through the aether much in the same way an earthworm moves through the soil, or a fruitworm through an apple. In each case a tunnel is left which marks the creature's passage. The aether is the wyrms' native element. They are no more harmed by passing through it than a bird is by flying through the air or a fish swimming through the water. (Of course this presumes that both air and water are free of pollution.)

Passage through a wyrmhole typically offers no lasting harm in the medical sense. It is most often an involuntary experience, which leaves those who have done so stranded. Fortunately, the aforementioned dedicants of Temporamancy make it their practice to rescue such stranded individuals. Black Grove Hospital maintains a Home for Temporally Displaced Persons.

Ventricular voyaging requires the construction of

a quantum ventricle, a chamber which, once energized, casts the occupants adrift in the temporal stream much in the same way a boat will come adrift if it is not securely moored. His Serene Highness Prince Calavicci described it as stepping out of the temporal stream and then back again so that "one voyages around time rather than through it."

Those desiring a greater understanding of these modes are welcome to seek it. Many fine works have been written on each. However, the purpose of this work is to provide a better understanding of the medical hazards of temporal transportation and how they may best be healed.

Maladies of the Mind

"Like the body, the mind requires wholesome nourishment, exercise and rest if it is to function in a healthy manner. Yet it remains a sad truth that, despite taking all the proper precautions, the mind remains vulnerable to infection and injury. Such is the condition of the human race in general, and no one person is superior for having not succumbed to a mental ailment to another who has. The mind is no less complex than the organ that it inhabits, and the forms and functions of both require

greater understanding from all. For the sufferings of the mind are no less real for being invisible than the air itself."

--Professor Exekiel Wood, T.W.F.M.A
Linacre Medical College, Oxford, 10.19.1868

In his lecture, Professor Wood emphasized that the maladies of the mind are no less deserving of compassion than the maladies of the flesh and should not be regarded as the result of some moral failing.

Many of these maladies are not restricted to temporal voyagers. Some foster motivation for it. Others are experienced in consequence of it. In the case of the former, proper treatment may well serve to prevent a person from taking that most perilous passage.

Regardless the medical community and the public at large would do well to follow the examples of Dr. Phillipe Pinel and the Society of Friends: treating those afflicted with mental illness with compassion and civil consideration as opposed to keeping them chained and confined which offers no clinical benefit whatsoever.

Far too many suffer in silence from otherwise treatable conditions in no small part due to the fear of being confined in such wretched institutions as Bedlam. It is the hope that this book will serve to educate and enlighten the general public with regard to the maladies of the mind.

Nostalgia Nervosa

Also known as Past Perfect Tension, this condition is generally rooted in a profound dissatisfaction with one's life. It generates a pervasive longing for the "good old days." This cancerous belief that "times were better then" frequently causes the sufferer to ignore the less pleasant aspects of the time period in question, such as the lack of hygiene, the prevalence of pestilence, and systemic distrust and suspicion of anything or anyone out of the ordinary.

On occasion, education may serve to dispel Past Perfect Tension as well as gentle yet firm reminders of all that there is to be enjoyed in the present. Psychoanalysis as well as a regimen of certain Svanic Tonics can help as well.

Avelocineurosis

This condition might best be described as impatience *in extremis*. It is also known as future perfect tension. Rooted in the belief that the future will prove better than the present, it often inspires individuals to take short-cuts to that time, that imagined Golden Age.

The biggest risk of course, is that there is no certainty as to what the future holds. There are a multitude of variables, perhaps the most complex of which is humanity itself. The forces of the natural world are likewise as yet beyond our full understanding. One may voyage to the future expecting a utopian paradise only to find a dystopian wasteland. The farther ahead one voyages, the greater the uncertainty.

Those who attempt to relieve their future perfect tension place themselves at risk of both Aftermath Anguish as well as Oneiroclassis Odynia or as it is more commonly called Broken Dreams Syndrome.

The best relief from FTP is to be found in doing one's best to improve the present. Certain Svanic Tonics may aid in that regard.

Pretermutavoma

This condition, also known as Past Imperfect Tension, is a desire to right some historical wrong (whether real or perceived) a belief that if past events can be altered, the present will be improved, even if only for oneself, in some cases, especially for oneself.

Unfortunately, as the Hillyer's Law decrees: voyaging into the past with the motive of changing it negates the possibility of success. Patients are then subject to Aftermath Anguish and Broken Dreams Syndrome.

In some cases, upon discovering that they are a *fatum ferramentum,* a tool of Destiny, patients suffer a form of an existential crisis.

Oneiroclassis
Odynia

Broken Dream Syndrome might best be likened to a form of bereavement with all its inherent emotions: anger, sorrow, melancholy, denial, and a sense of loss so profound as to be painful. It is not unique to temporal voyagers, but those who journey in the hope of witnessing some great event or meeting some great personage are particularly at risk.

Among historians and biographers there is an unfortunate tendency to glamourize their subjects: smoothing over rough edges, omitting unpleasant facts, and even exaggerating virtues and successes. This should not be considered a disparagement of their scholarship, for all too often these chronicles are commissioned by those who react poorly to what they perceive as criticism.

Yet these less than accurate depictions of past personages, places, and events can, and all too often do, leave the temporal voyager unprepared to cope with the unvarnished reality. Those who have been held up as paragons of one sort or another prove to be all too human with the faults and fallibilities of that condition.

In consequence of these disillusionments, admiration is often transmuted into abhorrence. Some patients will turn the force of their emotions inward, castigating themselves for folly.

Aftermath Anguish

Aftermath Anguish is the result of witnessing or experiencing some traumatic event. It is an all too common occurrence among those who have endured the horrors of combat be they military or civilian. Those afflicted suffer a blend of anxiety, melancholy, rage, and even guilt. A sight, a sound, even a smell can cause patients to recall the horrors of what they experienced. Not even sleep can bring relief, for these haunting memories are the very stuff of nightmares.

There cannot be enough emphasis on the fact that this malady is NOT a sign of weakness. Just as a physical blow bruises the flesh, an emotional blow bruises the spirit. The glories of battle are the invention of poets, as one gentleman learned when he set out to observe the French and English armies at Agincourt.

Patients are part-icularly anxious to avoid all

reminders of what they experienced, including persons, places, and pastimes. They often shun society in general, including that of family and friends. This generally compounds the patient's sense of isolation.

Such turbulence often provokes extremes: the most even-tempered of persons may burst into rage over the merest trifle, the most cautious may abandon all restraint, laughing one moment and then weeping the next.

It is not usual for these mental and emotional distresses to manifest in physical symptoms: trembling, ague, headaches, flutterings and tightness in the chest, and even shortness of breath.

All too often, patients succumb to despair, seeking relief in acts of self-destruction.

Symptoms can be relieved with Svanic Tonics, but the best form of treatment is therapeutic discourse with a qualified counselor and with fellow sufferers.

Megalgia Morosia

A form of Aftermath Anguish, this condition is suffered in consequence of the patient realizing that they have been used as a *fatum ferramentum*, a tool of Destiny. This tends to occur most often when the patient, who is already suffering from Pretermutavoma, discovers that they are responsible, if only in part, for the wrong that they meant to correct.

It can be especially traumatic when the incident in question involves one or more fatalities.

There are two primary phases of this condition: melancholy despair and manic desperation. Each patient will react differently. It is not unusual for a patient to swing from one to the other and back again to the detriment of their physical well-being.

Such a cycle is inherently unsustainable both physically and emotionally. Collapse, when it comes, is generally the best time to intervene and persuade the patient to seek treatment. Intervention is sometimes effective during the phase of melancholy despair, but should not be attempted during manic desperation. In that state of mind the patient will resist the very idea of treatment, and if confined, will repeatedly attempt escape. Sadly, too often when patients succumb to despair, they commit an act of self-annihilation.

When the patient is receptive, treatment consists

of a regimen of Svanic tonics,
counsel, and therapeutic discourse with fellow patients.

Maladies of the Flesh

There are certain obvious hazards attached to making a temporal voyage, perhaps the greatest of which is being unable to return to one's present. Others include:

- Materializing inside a solid object
- Having one's vehicle or vortex generator damaged, destroyed, or stolen

-Being accused, or worse, convicted of witchcraft
-Being suspected of godhood
-Being offered as a sacrifice
-Compulsory matrimony
-Being infected with an ancient pathogen

Even if a temporal voyager manages to avoid all contact with humans, there remain the risks of the natural world:

-Being consumed by a carnivore

- -Being injured or killed by a large herbivore
- -Being bitten or stung by some primordial insect or reptile
- -Being caught up in some seismic cataclysm
- -Being at the mercy of undocumented weather patterns

All the aforementioned hazards are such that any intrepid explorer may experience in the present time and the medical establishment is equipped to cope with them. Let us therefore turn our attention to the Temporal Related Injuries and Diseases that Black Grove Hospital was established to treat.

Chronokinetosis

Many persons find themselves unwell when they voyage over the water, through the air, or even over land on the railroad. It is no different when one is traversing the temporal stream, when the medium of voyage is time itself.

Such a voyage is a brutal assault upon the senses. Even the most intrepid of explorers can be afflicted.

SYMPTOMS

Critical:

Hiccups, blurred vision, giddiness

Dire:

Diarrhea, nausea, shortness of breath, vertigo

Extreme:

Synesthesia, clumsiness, loss of grammar

Symptoms are often more severe on the outbound trip than the return. Likewise voyaging to the past is less strenuous than voyaging to the future.

Medication is available to treat it, but if symptoms persist for more than two days, one should seek immediate medical assistance. Those prone to extreme cases are advised to take an able, trustworthy companion along on any temporal voyage.

Mnemonic Miscordinancy or Beckett Syndrome

This condition most commonly occurs as a result of long-term use of ventricular transport. For reasons as yet undetermined, the use of a quantum ventricle degrades the memory engrams in the brain resulting in their contents becoming jumbled or lost.

Because the most vulnerable engrams are the ones

containing the weakest and least used memories, the condition often does not become apparent until well past onset.

In the case of Professor Beckett, it was first noticed after he stormed into the office of the Dean of Talbot College, Cambridge University outraged that not a "single student could be bothered to attend my lecture this morning!"

The Dean calmly pointed out that as Professor Beckett was now a Fellow and not a Tutor, he no longer gave lectures. Dismayed, Beckett admitted to having trouble with his memory. The Dean arranged for Beckett to be examined by the mnemonic specialist Doctor Sven Suddigrumpa then a Fellow of Gifford Medical College whilst developing the Muninn Scale of Mnemonic Capability.

Fortunately Professor Beckett had volunteered for Dr. Suddigrumpa's study so there was already a baseline. Prof. Beckett had initially been rated at 7 on the Muninn Scale, the third highest. Two-score temporal voyages later his rating had dropped to 4. As Dr. Suddigrumpa put it, "It's incredibly rare to see such a miscordant memory in such an otherwise disciplined mind."

Mild and lightly moderate cases can be managed with Mnemonic Medicine, even arrested if the patient makes no more temporal voyages. Moderate to major cases can be managed but the condition will continue to worsen.

Once a patient drops below a 5 on the Muninn Scale, they are no longer considered legally competent and require the superintendence of a guardian.

Tachyon Toxalgia or Parker's Pathology

Miss Parker, desirous to be the first woman to make use of a temporal vortex, journeyed to the past to make the acquaintance of a certain royal lady.

Upon her return Miss Parker seemed despondent. It would appear that the lady in question did not satisfy Miss Parker's expectations. Yet while the diagnosis of Broken Dream Syndrome accounted for her mental condition, her physical one gave rise to concern.

Miss Parker exhibited an increased appetite as well as such weakness as made her unable to feed herself. She ate and slept, burned with fever and complained of the odor of pickled mushrooms, though no mushrooms, pickled or otherwise, were in her vicinity. Her once vibrant and thick hair dulled and thinned leaving her with such wispy tresses as an infant possesses.

Her blood was drawn and analyzed and revealed the presence of tachyons.

Tachyons exist all around us. They comprise a substantial portion of the aether. On the material plane of existence, they are diffuse and static, no more distinguishable to the unaided eye than the grains of salt in seawater.

However, temporal voyaging, particularly the use of the vorticular method, allows for the exposure to high concentrations of excited tachyons, something

that the human body was not
designed to endure.

SYMPTOMS
Critical:
Nausea, fatigue, hair loss,
luminescent urine, and olfactory hallucinations.

Dire:
Befuddlement, increased appetite and thirst, fever,
muscle aches, and bone pain.

Extreme:
Corporeal dissolution.
{Some have theorized that the
body does not in fact

dissolve, but that its atoms shift in such a way as to make the aforesaid body indiscernible by human senses.}

Ontological Obversion or Nelson Syndrome

Miss Nelson was performing the final inspection of a temporal vehicle when its pilot engaged the launch sequence. Miss Nelson was engulfed by the backwash of energies. When they had dispersed, she was rushed to Black Grove Hospital.

At first Miss Nelson seemed none the worse for the

mishap. She exhibited none of the symptoms of aether burn or tachyon toxalgia.

It must be noted that Miss Nelson had been born with a benign ocular ir-regularity: a blue left eye and a green right eye. When her vision was tested, the examiner noticed that the left eye was now green and the right blue. Furthermore Miss Nelson insisted the letters on the optotype had been printed backwards.

After a full battery of tests, it became apparent that Miss Nelson's entire being had been obverted, as though she had somehow switched places with her own looking-glass reflection.

Prior to the accident she had been left-handed, but during her recovery her friends noticed that she had begun to use her right. Yet apart from having to "learn to read and use tools all over again," she appeared to be essentially unscathed.

However appearances, as they often are, were deceiving. According to her friends, Miss Nelson made it a point to observe a balanced, wholesome diet, favoring fish and fowl over the heavier meats. Yet within a fort-night of the accident, she had lost over five stone and succumbed to a malaise that had confined her to her bed.

A postmortem examination revealed that her ability to absorb nutrients from food had been severely compromised.

Since then medicine has been developed to allow others afflicted with this condition to live largely independent of institutional care. However, it is much preferred that preventive measures such as protective shielding as well as keeping a distance of ten meters from any departing temporal vehicle. Chrononauts would also do well to advise their support staffs of the time and place of their return.

Corporeal Chronospasticity* or Detamble's Disorder

This condition mainly develops as a result of frequent ventricular voyaging though it has been known to occur with those who favor the use of vortices and even vehicles.

---

* This is not to be confused with such instances in which a mechanical or operational error causes a temporal voyager to arrive at somewhere and/or somewhen other than the desired destination.

Dr. Felicity Cosgrove

All creatures experience time at the same rate: minute by minute, hour by hour, etc. Our awareness of this passage can be, and frequently is, affected by our emotional states. Yet, barring the machinations of a Temporamancer, time neither speeds up or nor slows down. The pace of the temporal stream is as fixed as the pace of the moon's movement through its phases. However, with frequent trips, a temporal voyager's body can shift from being chronostatic to chronospastic.

In the case of Miss Detamble, she made a full two dozen temporal voyages over the eight weeks of the Long Vacation of Cambridge University. A librarian as well as an ardent historian, she set out with the intention of "solving history's mysteries."

This much is known thanks to a series of diaries she kept with a scholar's attention to detail. These diaries were discovered during the efforts of Cambridge University Librarian Bradshaw to catalog and organize the various books and manuscripts in the library's collection.

In one of these diaries she describes strolling through the gardens of Hampton Court Palace and how, between one step and the next, she "went from morning to evening, from being one in a crowd to being solitary." Drawn by the sound of raised voices she observed "a man in a cardinal's raiment arguing with a woman he addressed as 'Joan'."

Many belaureled historians have denounced Miss

Detamble's diaries as a hoax. (It may be of interest to note that her most fervent and vocal detractors are those whose theses she has challenged if not outright refuted.) Others have wondered at the significance of the numbering of the volumes. The Cambridge collection includes volumes one through twelve, fourteen through sixteen, eighteen, and twenty. There is much speculation regarding the missing three volumes, the leading theories being they were somehow destroyed, or remain secreted in some unknown location or other.

Those missing volumes are stored in the Black Grove Archives. In them she describes the instances in which she found herself moving about in time without the use of a vehicle, vortex, or ventricle.

"It feels like nothing so much as a jolt of static electricity, only involving my entire body as opposed to a single point of contact, yet there is no pain. There is also a sense of slight vertigo much as one

experiences when rising too swiftly after sitting for an extended period. If I had to put a word to it, the one I would choose would be 'spasm'."

Chronospasms are as involuntary as sneezes. It remains to be determined what triggers them. Until such time as the proper monitoring equipment can be scaled to a degree allowing it to be carried on the patient, we can only surmise as to the cause.

The inherent danger of chronospasms lies in the fact

that one can never be sure where or when a patient will manifest. Some patients are drawn to sites of prior visits thereby running the risk of encountering them-selves. Regardless, every patient is subject to the aforementioned risks of temporal voyaging without even the benefits of planning and supplies.

Fortunately, that is to say, in the scientific sense, while Miss Detamble is the first known case, she is no longer singular in that regard. Other cases, of varying degrees of severity have made it possible to form a body. of knowledge on this condition.

SYMPTOMS
Mild:
Displacement lasts from two minutes to twelve hours. Patients return after an absence of fifteen seconds to fifteen minutes. Patients are typically propelled to a temporal location they have previously visited.

Moderate:

Displacement lasts from twelve hours to twelve days. Patients return after an absence of thirty minutes to thirty hours. Patients are typically propelled to a temporal location they have previously visited, but not the same physical location, i.e. a patient who had previously visited the year 1588 to observe the defeat of the Spanish Armada, "spasmed" back to that same day but found himself aboard the *San*

Martín instead of the *Ark Royal.**

Major:

Displacement lasts for more than twelve days. As in the case of Miss Detamble, the patient's absence may be indefinite. Patients may be propelled anywhere or anywhen in the world.

TREATMENT

Mild:

Medication

---

* The voyager in question was able to escape before perishing in the conflict.

Moderate:

Medication, some patients have found meditation to be helpful as well.

Major:

Medication, although the dosage required presents a high risk of athanification. Research is being done on potential surgical implants. There has been limited success in housing patients in anchored quantum ventricles. Black Grove Hospital makes every effort to support these patients in comfort and dignity.

CAUTION:

While refraining from taking the prescribed medicine is certainly the right of an adult individual of sound mind, the consequence of not taking it may be very severe indeed, such as those mentioned in the introductory text of this section. Nor is it yet known if the condition is progressive.

Based on information provided by both the afflicted and non-afflicted, a minimum of seven days between temporal voyages is recommended to prevent this condition.

Arduspirosis or Lambert's Infirmity

    Mr. Lambert was first discovered on the roof of Black Grove Hospital swaddled in a blanket and hammock which suggested that he had arrived via the rapidly departing airship. His coughing and wheezing suggested he was afflicted with croup. He was administered vapor therapy which produced little relief. When he began expelling blood as well as black sputum, it was determined a lung lavage was needed.

The material flushed forth resembled nothing so much as diluted tar. A chemical analysis revealed it contained several common pollutants as well as compounds that defied efforts at identification, though they shared certain elements with gasoline and paraffin.

When asked, Mr. Lambert gave his profession as "a Temporal Gentleman Adventurer." He gave no details other than that he had voyaged to the distant future "in the hopes of finding my fortune." It should be noted that his responses were given in written form as his voice was all but gone and his chest muscles too sore to have allowed of speech regardless. After a fort-night he was discharged leaving with the promise to be more cautious in his explorations.

Some months later Mr. Lambert was again discovered on the beach of Black Grove Isle with tearing eyes sneezing as though his life depended on it. A sedative was administered and his nasal passages were flushed of a yellowish sort of slime. Analysis revealed the mucous contained the pollen of some two score different species, a good dozen of which were believed to be extinct.

When asked, Mr. Lambert would only say that as the future had proved too risky he had thought to seek his fortune in the distant past, though once again he would not admit to any particulars.

As Mr. Lambert's experiences illustrate, the

disparity in the composition of the atmosphere between different points in time can put a tremendous strain on the respiratory system. Voyaging to the pre-industrial past exposes the system to an absence of pollutants as well as higher concentrations of pollen. In voyaging to the future, one risks exposure to a higher degree of pollution as well as a greater or lesser degree of ionization in the air. The amount of available oxygen may also be less than that to which the patient may be accustomed

The consensus of the medical staff was that while Mr. Lambert had been the first, he would certainly not be the last. Therefore, research commenced at once on the remedy which is now called Respiratory Restoratives.

SYMPTOMS
Critical:
Sneezing, runny nose, watery eyes, and decreased hearing

Dire:

Persistent cough, shortness of breath, rapid pulse, florid complexion

Extreme:

Coughing blood, labored breathing, blurred vision, lightheadedness, loss of consciousness

TREATMENT
Critical:
Medication, aromatic vapor therapy

Dire:

Medication, flushing of the nasal passages, aromatic vapor therapy

Extreme:

Lung lavage, medication, aromatic vapor therapy

Aether Burn

Exposure to concentrated aether, particularly during a turbulent passage, can scorch the epidermis much in the same way as sunlight. This tends to occur most often while using an improperly shielded vehicle, though the support staffs of vorticular voyagers are also at high risk.

It can also occur when passing through aetheric turbulence. Chrononauts are advised to have reliable aetherometers installed in their vehicles. Aether readings should also be taken before generating a tachyon vortex.

SYMPTOMS
First Degree:
Blue, tingling skin; affects the outer layers of skin

Second Degree:
Blue tingling skin, opalescent blisters, wrinkling in much the same manner as when the skin is saturated with

water; affects all layers of skin

Third Degree:
Violet tingling skin, oozing opaline rash, fidgeting, mild euphoria; affects the skin and underlying tissues

Fourth Degree:
Transparent tingling skin, insomnia, restlessness, loss of appetite, exhilaration; affects the skin, deeper tissues and muscles.

TREATMENT

First Degree:

Wash the wound with distilled water, apply crème and bandages. Keep the dressing dry and change every 8 hours.

Second Degree:

Lance any blisters with a sterilized needle. Wash affected area with distilled water, apply crème and bandage. Keep the dressing dry and change every 4 hours.

Third and Fourth Degree:
Seek immediate medical help,
preferably from Black Grove
Hospital.

CAUTION:

When dressing an aether burn,
be sure NOT to touch the
affected area with one's bare
hands. Undyed silk gloves
should be used whenever
possible but cotton and
rubber will suffice when
combined with Epidural
Emulsion. If pus comes into
contact with bare skin, flush
the area with distilled water
at once. DO NOT ALLOW PUS TO

COME INTO CONTACT WITH ANY ORIFICE OR MUCOUS MEMBRANE! If, for some reason, pus is ingested, add salt to distilled water and gargle for no less than two minutes.

Distilled water MUST be used. Otherwise any metals, minerals, and microorganisms in the water will propagate within the patient's body requiring surgical excision.

Retinal Reversion

Also known as Aether Glare this condition causes the patient to perceive the world as being upside down which can have and adverse effect on the patient's balance causing them to experience vertigo.

According to the renowned oculist Dr. Ignatius Conrad Phaerries, the mechanics of human vision are such that the eyes indeed do perceive the world as being upside down, and it is due to the governing mechanisms in the brain that we see it the right way up. Looking at concentrated aether without any form of protection will cause these mechanisms to overload and shut down much in the same way any overloaded machine will do. Specially tempered goggles, when worn properly, will guard against it.

As yet there is no cure for this condition other than rest. A good night's sleep is often efficacious in reversing the reversion. For those whose impairment is permanent, Dr. I.C. Phaerries is developing corrective spectacles.

Chromatic Conversion

In this condition the patient's perception of colors is reversed: green grass will appear to be red, a yellow flower will appear to be purple and a blue sky will appear to be orange. Several patients who have experienced this condition have admitted to thinking they had somehow traveled to another planet or even to another dimension.

Chromatic conversion is the result of vorticular voyaging in distances of more than five hundred years without the use of proper eye protection. It often dissipates in less than an hour, faster with the use of the appropriate blinking and thinking exercises.

For those with more persistent symptoms, Dr. I. C. Phaerries has developed corrective spectacles.

Conjointure

Conjointure can happen during a collision or even during aetheric turbulence. Two or more persons become stuck together, not unlike the Bunker brothers.

Depending on the degree and complexity of the injury, it is often possible to separate the victims with surgery. On occasion it may be necessary for one patient to sacrifice a limb. Sadly, sometimes it is necessary for one to be sacrificed that the other may live. Though more often than not, it is possible, with appropriate physical and social therapy, for the patients to live meaningful lives while still conjoined.

Most frequently occurs during vorticular voyages however it can also happen with improperly shielded vehicles. In all fairness though the only way to guarantee it will not happen is to not voyage through time.

Dismogrification

Much like conjointure, dismogrification occurs most frequently during vorticular voyaging. When the patient arrives at their destination, their component atoms have recombined in such a way that the body does not conform to the anatomical standard. Typically this involves the limbs, arms being switched with legs and so forth.

As a general rule this condition is not fatal,

especially if the vital organs remain intact and inside the body. Then, as with conjointure, the problem can be corrected with surgery. In many cases patients require help in learning how to use their limbs again.

Autoancestry

A gentleman, whilst on an expedition to the past, dallied with a lady. (NOTE: It is NOT the intention of the author to cast any aspersions upon the character of any person laboring under this socially unfortunate condition.) Upon his return he became privy to certain family secrets. After making certain calculations he came to realize the highly likely possibility of him being his own maternal grandfather.

Given the disparity between the sexes with regard to the physical efforts of reproduction, it should be noted that while women are far less likely to suffer from direct autoancestry than men, they are by no means immune. A lady, whilst on an expedition to the past, dallied with a gentleman. Unwilling to expose an infant to the hazards of a temporal voyage she left the child to be placed for adoption. Upon her return she discovered that her son was also her grandfather.

With respect to the whys and wherefores of auto-ancestry, the author prefers to leave such matters to metaphysicians. What is of concern is the suffering of those who have discovered that they should be assigned more than one branch on the family tree. Too many consider autoancestry cause for shame which too often leads to melancholy. The discovery itself can often trigger Aftermath Anguish.

Autoancestry is the sort of phenomenon wherein the precept of the less knowledge, the less suffering pertains. The only prudent advice is to not inquire too closely into one's family history, and, upon discovery, to seek sympathetic counsel.

Pregnancy Problems

The amount of exertion
deemed appropriate for a
pregnant woman varies greatly.
A number of factors must be
considered. The predominant
one is often the woman's
position in society. Yet
with regard to such matters
as horseback riding,
gardening, domestic chores
and such what, it is best for
each expectant mother to be
guided by her local midwife.
That being said, it cannot be

emphasized enough, that if one wants to have a healthy family, one should not go on a temporal voyage.

This injunction is by no means exclusive to the female sex. The exact process by which human spermatozoa are produced remains a mystery and the effects of temporal voyaging on that process are even more mysterious. Only the results can be described: children who suffer from some variant of abnormal aging.

With regard to females, even those who are not yet pregnant when embarking on a temporal voyage are at risk for conceiving children who age abnormally. Those who are pregnant are also at risk for other hazards: fetal expulsion, fetal reversion, and fetal fixation.

Fetal expulsion, more commonly called a miscarriage, happens more often in vehicular and vorticular travel. (It cannot be emphasized enough, that embarking on a temporal voyage for the purpose of inducing a miscarriage is most unwise. There are better and safer methods available.)°

Unlike with the more common sort of miscarriage, with fetal reversion the cells implode until there are none left. Imagine the branches and roots of a tree being drawn back into the trunk and the trunk being drawn down into the ground becoming smaller and smaller until it is once again encapsulated into the seed from which it sprang.

° Black Grove Hospital and its affiliates provide treatment for "parasitic uterine growths". Your privacy will be respected.

Sometimes the seed may germinate again, but more often it does not.

Fetal fixation occurs when the tissues cease development altogether. Just as a flower nipped in the bud will never bloom, a fixated fetus will never mature. In rare instances, if the pregnancy is sufficiently advanced, it is possible to perform a Caesarian section and deliver a living child. Generally though, the pregnancy becomes parasitic in nature and must be terminated for the woman's well-being.

Abnormal Aging

    Abnormal Aging mostly afflicts the children of temporal voyagers although it is by no means limited to that group. Each case is unique but all can be sorted into one of four categories:

    1. Tachysaevia

    2. Bradysaevia

    3. Scalenaevia

    4. Enantisaevia

1.   Tachysaevia, or rapid aging, presents a great

hardship not in the least because the mind does not mature at the same rate as the body. What may seem to be an adult woman in peak condition may well turn out to be a rather young girl with little, if any, understanding of her body's desires.

Educating tachysaevic children can be challenging since most schools will not accept them. It is also difficult for them to form friendships, particularly since their greater strength and speed give them a supposedly unfair advantage in certain games. Nor does it help that by the time tachysaevic children are old enough to form meaningful friendships, they have already gone through so many of the experiences that serve as milestones on the road to maturity, i.e. the loss of their milk-teeth.

Yet for all the hardships, the greatest pain of tachysaevia invariably belongs to the parents who are doomed to outlive their children.

2. With bradysaevia, or slowed aging, what may usually take months or years, can take decades and even centuries. At first it may seem more a blessing than a burden: who among us wouldn't enjoy having all the benefits of youth for twice, even thrice as long as our natural allotment? Yet such a prolonged childhood does not come without cost. Children have no standing in our world, so a man of forty who has the appearance of being merely fourteen will not be allowed to act on his

own behalf but needs must find a proxy who will do so for him.

Yet, even if the Government and Society were prepared to make special dispensations, the fact remains that the bradysaevic will become bystanders as their friends age and succumb to the natural processes. Rather than racing ahead, they are left behind.

Many adopt a nomadic lifestyle, becoming emotional if not physical recluses. There are those who succumb to a sort of despairing debauchery to distract themselves from their loneliness.

3. Scalenaevia, or irregular aging, might best be described as having both of the aforementioned conditions concurrently. The luckiest ones are those whose cases follow a discernible mathematical pattern. These fortunate few can then plan for and around their rates of aging as the rapid portions tend to be both quite painful and fatiguing.

For too many, their rate of aging is unpredictable leaving parents and children aware that a "growth spurt" can occur at any time. This awareness often fosters both anxiety and melancholy. Since these episodes resemble nothing so much as an epileptic seizure, they are regarded as such by the ignorant. Given Society's less than enlightened consideration for those suffering from that ailment, it is no great wonder that the scalenaevic prefer to remain at home where they are

125

accepted rather than venturing into public.

4. An enantisaevic child ages backwards, rather than growing older, they grow younger, physically at least. Perhaps the one advantage these children have is that their condition is almost immediately apparent. That is to say, they may at first appear tachysaevic but within the first month or two of life, their physical condition will determine which they are.

This particular condition is relatively new, that is to say, only recently known in the medical community. It is possible that there have been enantisaevic persons in the past, yet given the nature of this condition, it is doubtful that any survived infancy. In the event that some did they would have had to become either nomadic or reclusive if not both for their own survival.

Regardless the study of this particular aging abnormality must be done with the utmost respect for the subject's sovereign rights as a person.

There has been some success in treating the first three conditions with medicine. With regard to the fourth it is currently beyond the power of medicine to intervene other than to offer refuge such as the Black Grove Asylum for the Aging Impaired.

Athanification

Patient enters a state of absevic homeostasis, neither aging nor sustaining injury, even those that would otherwise prove fatal. Such an existence is often lonely and subject to bouts of melancholy.

The condition is also dangerous. Many societies will not accept the athanificated into their midst and treat them with hostility born from ignorance and fear. Furthermore, they risk capture by unscrupulous persons for use in experimentation.

Remedies

The majority of the ingredients used in the medicines described in this volume are innocuous on their own. However, combining them without using the proper techniques is an extremely hazardous endeavor. The potential consequences in-clude, but are not limited to:

- -full body depilation
- -epidermal evaporation
- -osteoid liquefaction

-loss of any or all five
  senses
-partial or total
  lithofication
-partial or total
  paralysis
-death

Once again the author
and publisher hereby waive
any liability for the
irresponsible actions of
others.

Tachyon Tablets

USES:

Treatment for Tachyon Toxalgia. It binds to the
particles and expels them
from the body utilizing its
mechanisms for disposal of
waste. Patients should not
be concerned if they
experience:

- Dark urine
- Iridescent perspiration
- Opalescent stools
- Gritty tasting saliva

These are signs that the medicine is working.

CAUTION:

Do NOT take with liquor or other intoxicants. Do NOT take while pregnant or seeking to become so. This applies to males as well as females.

SIDE EFFECTS:
- -Restlessness^
- -Increased appetite and thirst
- -Persistent/Lingering taste of mint
- -Night-sweats

134

- Feelings of uncleanliness
- Feelings of ennui^
- Volatility of temper^

^Other patients have reported that these can be relieved by listening to music. The harp and the piano are particularly efficacious.

INGREDIENTS:
Angelica officinale, Ocimum basilicum, Citrus bergamia, Citrus, nobilis, Citrus paradisi, Cinnamom verum, Cinnamomum camphora, Cedrus deodara, Corylus avellana, Cuminum cyminum, Eucalyptus, Panax, Carya illinoinensis,

135

Foeniculum vulgare, Juglans,
Glycyrrhiza glabra, Salvia
lavandulaefolia, Myristica,
Origanum majorana, Origanum
vulgare, Mentha piperita,
Pimenta dioica, Heluchrysum
italicum, Salvia sclarea,
Salvia rosemarinus, Kunzite,
Citrine, Vanilla planifolia,
Dendrohaem, Ferrous silicate,
Rhodochrosite, Cervine lactum,
Ranine sanguis, Syzygium
aromaticum, Citharexylum cau-
datum Matricaria recutita,
Rhodonite, Onychinus,
Nephrite

Chronokinetosis Caplets

USES:

Alleviation of the symptoms of chronokinetosis. Dosage is determined by the temporal distances voyaged.

CAUTION:

Do not take with liquor or other intoxicants. Do not take with milk. Take with tea if possible or clean water.

SIDE EFFECTS:

- Perception of writing in three dimensions
- Photophobia
- Increased hearing acuity
- Aversion to pork
- Ambidexterity
- Increased agility
- Numbness in the nose

INGREDIENTS:
Zingiber officinale, Citrus bergamia, Citrus nobilis, Valerian, Lavandula, Mentha piperita, Mentha spicata, Glycyrrhiza glabra, Vanilla planifolia, Cedrus deodara, Salvia rosemarinus, Ocimum basilicum, Cinnamom verum, Foeniculum vulgare, Kunzite, Syzygium aromaticum, Equine lactum, Myristica, Anethum

graveolens, Nacre, Anserine sanguis, Sard, Chrysopogon zizanioides, Rhodochrosite, Elletaria Cardomomum, Beryl cyan, Rhodonite, Angelica officinale, Matricaria re-cutita, Dendrohaem, Ortho-clase, Magnesium hydroxide

Panacean Pills

USES:

By augmenting the immune systems of temporal voyagers, this medicine helps prevent outbreaks of exotic diseases.

CAUTION:

Do not take while pregnant or seeking to become so. This applies to males as well as females.

This medicine is far more effective for past diseases: the Black Death, sweating sickness, the Scotch pox, *et cetera*. These ailments are already known to the present medical establishment, whereas we can only speculate as to what manner of pathogens the future may produce. Those inclined to voyage to the future are advised to observe a quarantine for at least a fortnight upon their return. If they notice **any** symptoms they should immediately contact Black Grove Hospital's Plague Prevention Squad.

SIDE EFFECTS:

- -Compulsive tidiness
- -Aching bones
- -Fatigue
- -Alternating fever and chills
- -Cravings for broth and soup
- -Inappropriate bursts of laughter
- -Floral Flatulence

INGREDIENTS:
Murine sanguis Ursine Lactum, Matricaria recutita, Cinnamom verum, Syzygium aromaticum, Cedrus deodara, Glycyrrhiza glabra, Mentha piperita, Laurus nobilis, Echinacea, Citrona balzamo, Hyssopus officinalis, Lavandula, Carya

illinoinensis, Inula odorata,
Pyrite, Vanilla planifolia,
Citrus australasica, Thymus
serpyllum, Panax, Tagetes,
Eucalyptus, Origanum vulgare,
Melissa, Angelica officianle,
Cupressus simpervirens, Cori-
andrum sativum, Heluchrysum
italicum, Melaleuca quin-
quenervia, Santallum album,
Anacardium occidentale,
Corylus avellana, Dendrohaem,
Sanguilith, Agate (Botswana),
Hematite, Jaiet, Onychinus,
Quartz, Quartz (rutilated),
Tourmaline pepon, Tourmaline
viridis

Constitutional Capsules

USES:

Treatment for most types of abnormal aging by regu-lating the metabolism.

CAUTION:

DO NOT TAKE THIS MEDICINE WITHOUT A PRESCRIPTION! Do not take more than the prescribed dosage. Doing either carries a high risk of athanification.

Do not take with liquor or other intoxicants.

SIDE EFFECTS:

- -intolerance for spontaneity
- -Need for precise punctuality
- -Inability to gain or lose weight
- -Decreased rate of hair growth
- -Somnambulism
- -Pseudoplacidity
- -Affinity for needlework

INGREDIENTS:
Syzygium aromaticum, Cedrus deodara, Cinnamom verum, Matricaria recutita, Cyan beryl, Glycyrrhiza glabra, Mentha piperita, Eucalyptus,

Tritcum vulgare, Primula
vulgaris, Malachite, Salvia
rosemarinus, Lapine lactum,
Cygnine sanguis, Angelica
officionale, Prunis dulcis,
Dendrohaem, Juglans, Ana-
cardium occidentale, Sard,
Agate, Citrine, Amazonite,
Nephrite, Orthoclase, Onychinus, Quartz, Aluminum
fluoro-hydroxyl-silicate

Mnemonic Medicine

USES:
Treatment for Mnemonic Mis-cordinancy. It preserves (and in some cases restores) memory engrams in the brain. Dosage varies by age, cognitive capacity, and severity of symptoms.

CAUTION:

This medicine is meant to be taken **ONLY IN THE PRESCRIBED DOSAGE!** Taking more will prompt intermittent episodes of recall as well as cause dreams to be encoded as though they were waking experiences, and thus aggravating the patient's original condition. Taking less will cause syntax memory corrosion.

Taking this medicine without a legitimate need will make the person who does so vulnerable to experiencing a sensory triggered mnemonic cataclysm, e.g. the smell of onion soup will prompt the recall of every single instance one has smelled onion soup all at once. Such an episode overwhelms the conscious focus, thus putting the sufferer, and too often anyone in their immediate vicinity, in great danger.

Do not take while pregnant or seeking to become so. This applies to males as well as females.

Do not take with liquor or other intoxicants.

SIDE EFFECTS:
- -improved numeracy and linguistic acquisition
- -improved dexterity
- -prickling sensation in the scalp*

- -loss of sense of direction
- -hair thickening
- -inability to sleep in an enclosed space
- -lightheadedness*

*Consult a temporal physician if symptoms last more than an hour after taking Mnemonic Medicine.

INGREDIENTS:
Citrona balzamo, Gingko biloba, Cympobogon, Huperzine, Juglans, Panax, Salvia lavandulaefolia, Ametrine, Salvia rosemarinus, Barite, Pyrite, Calcite viridis, Chromium beryl, Quartz, Barrus lactum, Chrysolithus,

Fluorite, Hematite, Carya illinoinensis, Tourmaline pulleiaceus, Corvine sanguis

Blood Boluses

USES:

Purification and replenishment of blood. Most often used as a supplement to Tachyon Tablets, Panacean Pills, and Respiratory Restoratives.

CAUTION:

Do not take with liquor or other intoxicants. Do not take while pregnant or seeking to become so. This applies to males as well as females.

SIDE EFFECTS:
- Fatigue
- Malaise
- Cravings for beef, the rarer the better
- Preference for being in sunlight*
- Increased thirst and urination
- Intolerance for fatty foods
- Tendency to speak in an iambic meter

*Patients should be allowed to sleep while in the sun,

but they should also be watched to avoid sunburn. Black Grove Hospital's Matron of Solar Therapy recommends alternating 15 minutes of sun with 30 minutes of shade.

INGREDIENTS:
Matricaria recutita, Mentha piperita, Cinnamom verum, Syzygium aromaticum, Cedrus deodara, Glycyrrhiza glabra, Vanilla planifolia, Salvia lavandulaefolia, Origanum majorana, Prunis dulcis, Myristica fragrans, Pyrite, Cupressus sempervirens, Citharexylum caudatum, Jug-lans, Dendrohaem, Eucalyptus, Sanguilith, Ferrous silicate, Aluminum Oxide, Quartz (rutiliated), Tourmaline viridis,

Nephrite, Lupine lactum,
Notilionine sanguis,

Transposition Troches

USES:

Treatment for Nelson Syndrome. It binds to the essential vitamins and facilitates their absorption by the body. Dosage is determined by patient's age and weight.

DIRECTIONS:

Just prior to eating, a troche should be placed under

the tongue and allowed to dissolve.

CAUTION:

DO NOT TAKE THIS MEDICINE UNLESS DIRECTED TO BY A *LICENSED* TEMPORAL PHYSCIAN! Taking it in the hopes of losing weight can and HAS PROVEN FATAL! There are safer methods available. Anyone seeking to lose weight should consult a reputable doctor as to the best method for them.

Do not take with liquor or other intoxicants.

SIDE EFFECTS[*]:

- An increased preference for fruits and vege-tables
- Feelings of languor for up to an hour after eating
- Intolerance for tobacco and snuff
- Increased olfactory acu-ity
- Renewed preference for human milk
- Preference for fish

---

[*] When seeking relief from side effects, please consult with your physician or pharmaceutical chemist as to which forms are most prudent.

-Dandification regarding
to personal hygiene

-Obsession with the
weather

INGREDIENTS:
Glycyrrhiza glabra, Cedrus
deodara, Juglans, Nephrite,
Eucalyptus, Cinnamom verum,
Matricaria recutita, Prunis
dulcis, Mentha piperita,
Mentha spicata, Vanilla
planifolia, Cuminum cyminum,
Pimpinella anisum, Syzygium
aromaticum, Citharexylum
caudatum, Ocimum basilicum,
Anethum graveolens, Citrine,
Elletaria cardomomum, Sard,
Citrus reticulate, Pimenta
dioica, Coriandrum sativum,
Citrona balzamo, Citrus
vulgaris, Origanum majorana,
Origanum vulgare, Viola
sororia, Dendrohaem, Carya

illinoinensis, Cymbopogon martinii, Arachis hypogaea, Cananga odorata, Carnelian, Achillea millefolium, Beryl cyan, Aventurine viridis Tourmaline pepon, Obsidian, Malachite, Anacardium oc-cidentale, Azurite, Ortho-clase, Rhodonite, Vulpine lactum, strigine sanguis,

Respiratory Restoratives

These pills come in separate shades for their separate uses: light for cleaner air, dark for dirtier air.

USES:
Treatment of critical and dire cases of Arduspirosis. It aids in relaxing the bronchial muscles and retaining oxygen that would otherwise be exhaled.

CAUTION:

THIS MEDICINE IS MEANT TO TREAT ACUTE CASES ONLY! AND SHOULD NOT BE TAKEN FOR MORE THAN A FORTNIGHT! An excess of oxygen can prove just as fatal as a shortage of it, albeit in a different manner. Patients who experience nausea, a ringing in the ears or tunnel vision should stop taking this medicine immediately.

Do not take while pregnant or seeking to become so. This applies to males as well as females.

SIDE EFFECTS:
- -Intolerance for cloying scents
- -Fear of flowers
- -Agitation
- -Compulsion to fan oneself
- -Inability to spell
- -Inability to sleep while prone
- -Tactile agnosia, specifically an inability to distinguish textures

INGREDIENTS:

Matricaria recutita, Cedrus deodara, Cinnamom verum, Syzygium aromaticum, Laurus

nobilis, Pimpinella anisum,
Glycyrrhiza glabra, Mentha
piperita, Callais, Vanilla
planifolia, Boswellia Sacra,
Cympobogon, Cinnamomum camphora, Eucalyptus, Myrtus
romanifolia, Origanum majorana, Delphine lactum,
Cupressus sempervirens, Heluchrysum italicum, Citrus
vulgaris, Citrine, Ravensara,
Hyssopus officeinalis, Juni-
perus virginiana, Rhodonite,
Origanum vulgare, Melaleuca
quinquenervia, accipitrine
sanguis,

Locking Lozenges

USES:

This medicine is used to treat Corporeal Chrono-spasticity by affixing the mind and body to the here and now.

CAUTION:

DO NOT TAKE THIS MEDICINE UNLESS DIRECTED TO DO SO BY A LICENSED TEMPORAL PHYSICIAN! Doing so will almost certainly cause the patient to enter into a paralithomorphic state and thus become a prisoner in their own body. They would be unable to move or speak yet fully aware of their own surroundings, capable of thought and feeling but unable to communicate.

SIDE EFFECTS[*]:

- Increased awareness of the passage of time.
- Feelings of heaviness
- Stiffness of the joints and muscles.

---

[*] When seeking relief from side effects, please consult with your physician or pharamcuetical chemist as to which forms are most prudent.

-Insomnia

-Heightened kinesthesia

-Bouts of languor

-Increased olfactory acu-
  ity

Risk of athanification

INGREDIENTS:
Cinnamom verum, Dendrohaem,
Mentha piperita, Matricaria
recutita, Cedrus deodara,
Syzygium aromaticum, Agate,
Vanilla planifolia, Citrine,
Sard, Silicon dioxide (tran-
sparent), Amazonite, Aven-
turine, Trochildine sanguis,
Rhodochrosite, Lynsine lactum

Aether Burn Crème

USES:
Treatment for first and second degree aether burns. Soothes the injured tissues and stimulates the body's own healing mechanisms.

DIRECTIONS:
Rinse affected area with distilled water. Apply crème until no more can be absorbed into the skin. Apply dressing and keep it dry.

CAUTION:
DO NOT TAKE ORALLY! Keep away from the eyes! If crème gets into eyes, rinse with DISTILLED WATER! If crème is swallowed, SEEK MEDICAL ASSISTANCE WITHOUT DELAY!

INGREDIENTS:
Aloe vera, Styrax benzoin, Pinguicula, Daucus carota sativus, Virago officinalis, Mazoil, Dalmaticum, Jojoba Oil, Melaleuca leucadendra, Melaleuca quinquenervia, Lavandula, Rosa damascene, Pogostemon cablin, Sesamum indicum, Prunis dulcis oil, Tritcum vulgare, Dendrohaem, Amazonite

Epidural Emulsion

USES:
Forms a monolayer on the skin which protects against damage by exposure to concentrated aether, sun-light, pollutants, and other irritants

DIRECTIONS:
Apply liberally to exposed skin. Protection breaks down after 15 minutes to an hour, especially if user has been engaged in strenuous exertions.

CAUTION: DO NOT TAKE ORALLY!
Keep away from the eyes! If emulsion gets into eyes, rinse with DISTILLED WATER! If emulsion is ingested, induce vomiting and SEEK MEDICAL ASSISTANCE WITHOUT DELAY!

INGREDIENTS:
Prunus armeniaca, Daucus carota sativus, Mazoil, Dalmaticum, Prunis dulcis oil, Cympobogon, Jojoba Oil, Pogostemon cablin, Sesamum indicum, Tritcum vulgare

Omniserum Ointment

USES:

Multi-purpose salve for the treatment of the stings and bites of primordial insects, arachnids, and reptiles.

DIRECTIONS:

After cleaning the wound apply a small amount and bandage. Be advised that additional treatment is recommended.

If at all possible, patients are requested to

bring a specimen to Black Grove Hospital for a more detailed analysis and treatment.

CAUTION:

This medicine is intended as an emergency measure to prevent immediate death. If possible, contact Black Grove Hospital's Temporal Evacuation Team for rescue.

DO NOT TAKE ORALLY! If emulsion is ingested, induce vomiting and SEEK MEDICAL ASSISTANCE WITHOUT DELAY!

INGREDIENTS:
Prunus armeniaca, Virago officinalis, Daucus carota

sativus, Citronella oil,
Citrona balzamo, Melaleuca
leucadendra, Rosa damascene,
Echinacea, Citrus vulgaris,
Jojoba oil, Cympobogon,
Dalmaticum, Mazoil, Salvia
lavandulaefolia, Cymbopogon
martini, Myristica fragrans,
Commiphora myrrha, Melissa,
Melaleuca quinquenervia,
Pogostemon cablin, Thymus
serpyllum, Sesamum indicum,
Prunis dulcis oil, Tagetes,
Viola sororia, Tritcum
vulgare, Lavandula

Svanic Tonics

The Tonics are named in honor of herbalist Svana Eirvinur. The powders are blended according to need, and brewed with soft apple cider and honey. They can be served chilled if that is favorable to the patient.

CAUTION:

DO NOT TAKE WITH ALCOHOL OR ANY OTHER INTOXICANTS!

Dr. Felicity Cosgrove

	Stimulant	Relaxant
Physical	Hvetja	Sefa
Mental	Útskýra	Sljór
Emotional	Æsandi	Róandi

Adunalum

EFFECTS:
Helps to prompt the patient to take action towards improving their own lives if not the world in general.

USES:
Nostalgia Nervosa, Megalgia Morosia, Avelocineneurosis, Melancholy Despair

BEST TAKEN:
First thing in the morning, then as needed throughout the

day.   Should not be taken at
least two hours before bed.

INGREDIENTS:

Hvetja, Útskýra, Æsandi

Aladunum

EFFECTS:

Helps to calm the passions and clarify the thoughts so that the patient acts from rational motives

USES:

Avelocineneurosis, Megalgia Morosia, Nostalgia Nervosa, Pretermutova, Oneiroclassis Odynia, Aftermath Anguish

BEST TAKEN:

Right after breakfast, then every three hours as needed.

Should not be taken two hours before bedtime. Do NOT take on an empty stomach!

INGREDIENTS:

Hvetja, Útskýra, Róandi

Amunadul

EFFECTS:
Helps to pull patients out of
their own minds and take time
to enjoy the world around
them.

USES:
Bradysevia,   Oneiroclassis
Odynia,   Nostalgia   Nervosa,
Avelocineneurosis,   Megalgia
Morosia, Aftermath Anguish

BEST TAKEN:
With every meal except for
supper. Do NOT take on an

empty stomach.

INGREDIENTS:

Hvetja, Sljór, Æsandi

Dualunam

EFFECTS:

Helps to soothe patients whilst prompting them into wholesome activity

USES:

Avelocineneurosis, Megalgia Morosia, Nostalgia Nervosa, Aftermath Anguish, Auto-ancestry, Oneiroclassis Odynia

BEST TAKEN:

An hour after each meal except for supper

Dr. Felicity Cosgrove

INGREDIENTS:

Hvetja, Sljór, Róandi

Dulamaun

EFFECTS:
Helps to soothe the patient in body, mind, and heart, especially when they are caught in the throes of hysteria. When diluted it also serves as an excellent aid to sleep.

USES:
Aftermath Annguish, Manic Desperation, Oneiroclassis Odynia, Megalgia Morosia, Autoancestry

BEST TAKEN:

As needed, should not be taken more than three times a day.

INGREDIENTS:

Sefa, Sljór, Róandi

Mudualam

EFFECTS:

Helps to cut through the distractions that patients employ to avoid examining their feelings.

USES:

Aftermath Anguish

BEST TAKEN:

First thing in the morning and an hour before each meal.

INGREDIENTS:

Sefa, Sljór, Æsandi

Nauladum

EFFECTS:

Helps to calm patients into a more rational frame of mind. They are less prone to reacting out of passion and conducting themselves in a more restrained and rational manner.

USES:

Avelocineneurosis, Megalgia Morosia, Nostalgia Nervosa, Pretermutova, Oneiroclassis Odynia, Aftermath Anguish, Autoancestry, Tachysevia

BEST TAKEN:

As needed, should not be taken more than four times a day.

INGREDIENTS:

Sefa, Útskýra, Róandi

Umalandum

EFFECTS:

Helps to calm the patient while making them more amenable to the benefits of therapeutic discourse.

USES:

Pretermutova, Oneiroclassis Odynia, Megalgia Morosia, Avelocineneurosis, Auto-ancestry, Nostalgia Nervosa, Aftermath Anguish

BEST TAKEN:

With each meal, Should not be taken on an empty stomach.

INGREDIENTS: Sefa, Útskýra, Æsandi

Afterword

Following the recovery of Miss Parker, it became clear that the medical establishment was ill-equipped to cope with the injuries and diseases associated with temporal voyaging. I therefore set out to become a Doctor of Pharmaceutical Chemistry as well as Medicine. My partner surgeon Mr. Edward Blackstone began a course of research and study to further develop and refine the requisite techniques for treating conjointure and dismogrif-ication.

Upon receiving our new credentials we applied for and were granted license to practice Temporal Medicine and Surgery. It was shortly afterwards that we opened Black Grove Hospital on the Isle of the same name. We are proud associates of the League of Intrepid Travelers and Explorers.

Furthermore, Black Grove Hospital is dedicated to research and education, hence the publication of this book.

If reading it has dissuaded anyone from risking the hazards of a temporal voyage, so much the better. For those who persist in transporting themselves in, through, and around time, it is to be hoped that they shall make their voyages better informed about the perils of such a passage.

Regardless the staff of Black Grove Hospital for Temporal Related Injuries And Diseases are always ready to provide the highest standard of care to those who need it.

Dr. Felicity Cosgrove

Whatever the condition, we
have pills for that.

About the Author

Felicity Jane Cosgrove spent her early years on her family's estate in New Zealand. At the age of 20 she received a First Degree in Botany from Elizabeth College, Oxford University. She then went on to study at Linacre Medical College, also at Oxford Univeristy.

She would later achieve a Doctorate of Pharmaceutical Chemistry, and open Black Grove Hospital along with her partner the surgeon Mr. Edward Blackstone.

Dr. Cosgrove is hailed as the Founder of Temporal Medicine.